GW01458376

30130505766427

The Coastal Guardians Go Scuba Diving

JOHN L. JEWELL

authorHOUSE®

AuthorHouse™ UK
1663 Liberty Drive
Bloomington, IN 47403 USA
www.authorhouse.co.uk
Phone: 0800.197.4150

© 2018 John L. Jewell. All rights reserved.

No part of this book may be reproduced, stored in a retrieval system, or
transmitted by any means without the written permission of the author.

Published by AuthorHouse 02/23/2018

ISBN: 978-1-5462-8929-6 (sc)
ISBN: 978-1-5462-8928-9 (e)

Print information available on the last page.

Any people depicted in stock imagery provided by Getty Images are
models, and such images are being used for illustrative purposes only.
Certain stock imagery © Getty Images.

This book is printed on acid-free paper.

Because of the dynamic nature of the Internet, any web
addresses or links contained in this book may have changed
since publication and may no longer be valid. The views
expressed in this work are solely those of the author and do
not necessarily reflect the views of the publisher, and the
publisher hereby disclaims any responsibility for them.

THE COASTAL GUARDIANS GO SCUBA DIVING

J ust one more gloriously carefree week on the coast and then Chalky White, Sue, and their parents would vanish. Vanish to resume their robotic lives in the suburbs of south London. It was such a different world to this quiet haven on the coast. The noise of the traffic, the hustle-and-bustle as city life reinstated its grip upon those who returned from such joyous and carefree days far from the hub of commerce, bit deep into the soul of a senior accountant.

When Mr. White was at work, he passed seemingly endless days in an office with a window overlooking the featureless brick wall of a neighbouring building; not that he had much time to gaze at the view!

Returning to work was always hard for him after the time he enjoyed during his holidays. In the city, he had few people he called friends, they were acquaintances or colleagues, unlike the Ross family. With them, his holidays were a time of freedom, exploration, and excitement. They were hard earned times to rest and relax after the stresses of work commitments. He wished he could spend every day at the cove, sail aboard the boats, or just float lazily upon the tidal estuary waves … He had enquired if the coastal town had a need for his services as an insurance broker, but he got little positive response. He was very good at his job, but the town council and the local business owners preferred to stay with their current insurers, the ones they had been with for so many years. To Mr. White, they were all being ripped-off by their loyalty. He could get them much better insurance coverage for far less money than they paid now. The sleepy coastal town did not recognise the highly competitive world in which he worked.

★ ★ ★

This was a clear, fine day near Summer's end. A closing of the time spent in good company, a time the White and the Ross families would relish and not hurriedly forget.

Aboard Mr. Ross's boat, he said, 'Good! You are all wearing lifejackets, but make sure you have flares to hand Michael! We are heading to deep waters.'

'I have them Dad! Where are we going to dive?' the boy asked excitedly as he fastened the neck of his wetsuit.

He had dived many times with his father and snorkelling was one of his favourite pursuits, this was his seventeenth dive as a scuba diver. He loved the comforting sensations of the deep water and he felt as one with it ... This time, his young brother Jamie, his friend Chalky and his father, (both had only scuba-dived once before) joined Mike and his father for the dive. Mr. Ross went through the important procedures of watching the time and the gauges and the signals they should use for emergencies. He checked the straps of each harness holding the tanks upon their backs and reminded them to check the tubes for air leaks once they entered the water.

'This is not a summer jaunt my friends, this is very serious, lives could be at risk if you ignore me. I want you to enjoy the experience and return safely to the boat,'

Mr. Ross said to his companions. 'Obey me at all times because I will be watching you, Michael will watch you as well,' the experienced sailor added.

Also aboard the boat were the wives of Mr. Ross and Mr. White, and his daughter Susan.

'Can I dive with you Daddy?' the young girl asked excitedly.

'Perhaps at another time, Susan. This is only my second dive and I don't feel confident to teach you yet. You see, I am learning just as your brother is; we are not proficient like Mr. Ross or Mike. If they are watching us, who will watch and teach you?' Mr. White replied.

'It's not fair! Boys have all the fun and girls just get to watch,' Susan said sulkily.

'Susan,' said Mr. Ross in a gentle manner, 'we have no spare wetsuits nor tanks. Mr. Parker does not stock wetsuits in your size because there is no demand for ones so young—'

'I don't need a wetsuit ... but you have two tanks and you could give one to me—'

Peter Ross smiled at the girl and said, 'why do you think we wear wetsuits, for the fashion, for the reputation we gain if others see us wearing them? Susan, dearest. They are to protect us from the intense cold of the deep water where the sun does not reach with its warming rays. As for the tanks? Yes, I do have two tanks, but not because I am greedy. As the experienced diver, I have responsibilities to my group. If the other divers get into trouble I have the spare tank which can save their lives and mine. If your parents bring you next year, you will have grown a little and I am sure that we could find a wetsuit for you. Now, could you lift that tank for me Susan and put it over there please, up onto that box so that you can attach it to Jamie's harness? Diving is about working together as a team and it is never too soon to learn if you wish to learn to dive.'

The girl struggled with the heavy tank, she dragged it slowly to the box but could not lift it from the deck. Everyone watched and admired her spirit as she strained futilely at the tank, her will demanded that she would do as her friend Mr. Ross had asked. Peter took the tank from her and strapped it swiftly to his son's back. 'What stopped you from doing what I just did Susan?' he asked casually.

'It is so heavy. So very heavy I could not lift it—' Susan began.

'When you dive Susan, you must lift the tank because you take that weight upon your back. Do you see now what diving involves, strict rules, strength, discipline, and teamwork? Below us lies another world, a world of peace and calm, a world of colours, sensations, and dangers not found above water. I do not wish to curb your enthusiasm to see that world, but you need one-to-one tuition to appreciate it as you should in all its glory. Next summer I will give you that tuition and you have my promise. Michael and James might also teach you and you can play together in the shallower waters. When I see that you are ready, I will take you to deeper waters ... but do not think that you will carry two tanks. I will do that, and I will watch as you learn and enjoy with my boys. I foresee a time when you might carry two tanks, but let me warn you, two tanks are no match for an ocean in torment, an ocean that screams its woes to the sky is one of the most ferocious of nature's creations. Along with hurricanes, earthquakes, and tidal waves. Do you know what the weather will be tomorrow Susan? Mr. Ross asked.

'No. And why should I worry about tomorrow?' Susan answered.

'Why indeed? Why should we worry if the sun may shine or hailstones drive us to ground? We could take the boat out and face the raging storm just for the fun of it, just to defy it and say, 'throw all you have at me, give me your worst and you cannot beat me because I am the best' … The remains of such fools litter the seabed, sometimes heroic fools, but fools nonetheless. Anyone who pitches against the sea is a fool and I have seen good men die in the ocean swells and they were not all fools, they died trying to help others in distress. It is our duty to help others because none of us can defeat the oceans, in that respect, we are all equal, captain or subaltern, petty officer or deck-hand. The sea recognises not the ranks we bestow because it is all powerful. Not one body of water ranks above another, no river, lake, nor ocean claims supremacy, and yet they are equally supreme. These words are to remind you of the safeguards we must take when we sail, we swim, and when we dive.'

Turning to the divers he said, 'Take this length of rope and link yourselves together with it. If you meet any problem, tug the rope to tell the next person on the line. And if you feel the tug, you must respond and warn the others along the line. You know the signals, so let us dive,' said Mr. Ross like a true sailor.

★ ★ ★

Mike tumbled backwards into the blue water and then looked up at his charges, calling them into the water one at a time. He checked for leaks in Mr. White's equipment and Chalky's also, then he got Mr. White to check his own equipment. Confident that they would follow his son, Peter Ross watched from behind the group. Mike herded the swimmers behind him, looking back constantly and supported by his father following and watching. He checked his watch because the timing is important when your life depends upon a single tank of oxygen.

They swam around the inviting soft and gentle waving fronds of the vast seaweed forest to avoid becoming entangled; Mike recalled his first dive when he had strayed into that kelp forest of seaweed. He had felt a sense of panic until his father guided him from the waving kelp fingers that seemingly grasped and grabbed him.

The divers swam around for some time enjoying the brilliant colours about them and the alien terrain ... until—

'Over there!' Mike shouted as he pointed, he realised that his companions could not hear his excitable words underwater. He had seen something protruding from a sandy patch amongst the jagged rocks on the seabed and he went to investigate. The group followed him to find out what had caught his attention ... Peter Ross checked his watch and the pressure gauge.

Streams of bubbles rose to the surface as the group removed handfuls of sand from around the buried object. 'Dad! It's a canon! Like the ones they had aboard those old galleons!' Mike exclaimed.

Peter Ross understood the muffled words because he could see for himself the muzzle of the tube ... He pointed to his watch and the gauge, saying that they should return to the boat.

★ ★ ★

Once the group was aboard, they removed their tanks and Peter stowed them in the lockers whilst Mrs. White unpacked the lunch.

'Dad! What about the canon? It would be great for the museum, or in front of the town hall, once it's cleaned up—' began Mike.

'Who is going to lift it, Michael? It must be very heavy indeed, much too heavy for my boat … we need some heavy lifting gear like Mr. Parker has at the chandlery. The trouble is, that once word gets out we will have every treasure hunter in the country descend upon this coast. We must keep this find a secret until we have explored the surrounding area, there could be a ship, more canons, or other relics, who knows what might be down there?' said Mr. Ross.

'What about your old friends in the navy, surely they have lifting gear?' Mr. White suggested.

'They do, but they would have more important things to attend to than an old canon. Besides, I was not a high-ranking officer when I left the navy and I do not have the kind of contacts needed for an operation of this kind … Wait a moment! Henry Winterton is on the town council, he was a senior naval officer I believe. Should we chance to ask him? We must inform the council at some point … No! not just yet. Michael, keep your wetsuit

on, we will dive again after lunch and see if we discover anything more down there.'
As Mr. Ross spoke, he had been tying a length of rope to a red marker buoy. 'To avoid attention to this spot, we will move the boat and sail around the bay returning to just above the canon where I will drop this marker. If we need to return tomorrow we can easily find the spot,' he added.

★ ★ ★

With the plates washed and stowed in the lockers, the two men readied the sail. 'To starboard!' said Mr. Ross as the anchor chain clattered on the metal guard.

The two brothers obeyed instantly whilst Chalky watched the well-rehearsed routine. The boat glided smoothly upon soft, silver-gilded waters as light cloud partly obscured the sun.

With the circuit of the bay done, Mr. Ross calculated the position of the canon and dropped anchor. 'I have checked the tanks and you have a maximum of one hour. Michael, Mr. White, and Chalky will dive with you, James will dive with me when you return. 45 minutes Michael! Not a minute more, just in case the gauges are faulty, is that clear?'

'Yes, Dad. 45 minutes only,' Mike said as he adjusted the timer on his diving watch.

'If you find anything, do not get excited about it, stay calm and make a mental note of what and where. If you get excited you will use up the oxygen faster, so keep checking the gauge. Take these bags with you for any small items of interest that you might find,' Mike's father told him.

Peter Ross handed the weighted end of a rope to Mr. White and said quietly, 'keep hold of this and let it go when I tug on it, that is the signal to return in case Michael loses track of time.'

Mr. White winked with a slight tilt of his head.

★ ★ ★

Down they went into deep magical blue waters, noticing the beautiful colours of the fish surrounding them contrasting against the green backdrop of the kelp forest. Mike's father had judged the spot perfectly, the boat was directly above the old canon.

Chalky was the first to signal, he held up what looked like a large crucifix ... and then his father found items of cutlery scattered in all directions. The boys helped him to gather as many as they could stuff into the bags ... Mike checked his gauge and his watch and signalled to Mr. White and Chalky, 'Ten minutes more!' he said, holding out all ten fingers and pointing to his watch.

★ ★ ★

Once back on board, the divers showed everyone their haul.

'Wow! This cutlery is silver! Look here where I rubbed it!' said Doris Ross.

Peter Ross turned his attention to the cross-shaped item so encrusted with barnacles, he glimpsed glinting reds and greens between the rough edges of the shells. He was sure that it was a crucifix of the kind he had seen in Catholic churches. Peter emptied a crate holding spare ropes and placed the finds into it. Mike had removed his wetsuit and now stowed the ropes away for safety.

Armed with the empty bags, Jamie and his father tumbled backwards into the water watched eagerly by their friends and family.

Peter followed the rope of the marker and checked his gauge when they reached the seabed, he checked Jamie's also.

Father and son scrambled around in the soft sand a few yards from where Mr. White had found the cutlery. Peter could see James becoming excited and drew closer as the boy held up a coin. Peter signalled to him to put it in the bag as they continued their search.

★ ★ ★

Later, aboard the boat, Peter Ross said, 'Have we got a surprise for you! Just look at this!' With a flourish, he emptied the contents of the two bags onto the deck, the four children scrambled to recover coins as they began to roll away across the deck.

'Peter! There must be over two hundred coins—' Mr. White began.

Mr. Ross interrupted, 'and there are more down there my friend, cutlery, salvers … we could not bring them all up. I suggest we return tomorrow with fresh tanks. We could tie sacks to ropes and haul the artefacts up … I wonder what the legal position is for treasure found at sea? Is it classed as treasure trove? I must ask Travis at the museum.'

The group cleaned the coins very carefully, although some were in mint condition.

'These are not English coins, I think they might be Spanish or Portuguese. They could even be from South America,' said Mr. White.

'That's true. Some of these are silver and some are gold, I think ... we might have a small fortune here ... do you think they might be what they called doubloons?' Peter asked.

Mike studied a coin in perfect condition and said excitedly, 'Dad! This could be King Ferdinand II and Queen Isabela I of Spain, we did this period in history! They got a special dispensation from the pope so they could marry because they were second cousins. She was 18 and he was 17 when they married in 1469—'

'Why do they teach you Spanish history at school?' Chalky interrupted.

'Well, you see Chalky, their daughter Catherine married Arthur, the Prince of Wales, but he died very young, and then she married his brother when he became King Henry the eighth of England. She was Catherine of Aragon, the youngest of Isabela's five children. I am sure that these coins are doubloons; look at the words around the edge ... I can see Ferdinand there and Isabella on the other side. These could be over four-hundred years old! Wow! I am holding a coin that few have touched in four hundred years ... But how do they come to be here Dad?' asked Mike.

'Your guess is as good as mine my boy. The fifteenth century was a time of great voyages to unknown lands, Christopher Columbus for example. The explorers were mostly Spanish and Portuguese at that time, but the British earned a reputation for piracy upon the high seas along with French and Maltese sailors. They would await the returning ships and attack them, often taking the ships as part of the prize. It could be that this haul is from a Spanish or a Portuguese galleon. The ship could be down there where we found this treasure, the crew might have been caught out by the wreckers who unwittingly sank a stolen ship. My mind creates so many scenarios from the words of my son and the feel of the coins … The lives lost to fortunes that the sea has held close for so many years. Love, friendship, and humanity are worth so much more than gold and silver. We will use this haul for the good of the town because although we found it, it is not rightly ours. Keep a coin each one of you, to remind us of this day and the friendships we share, the rest shall contribute towards this coast where we found them, and tomorrow we will dive again. Susan, can you gather-up the rascally coins that tried to escape back to the sea? Choose your favourite to stay with you for the rest of your life. It is yours, but you must never speak of it, where we found it or however many we may still find. We are The Coastal Guardians and secrets must play a great part in our plans for this coast. Are you with me? Can you keep secrets that others may try to glean from you?' Peter Ross enquired.

'What is glean … I don't know that word, Mum—' began Susan.

'Mia culpa,' said Mr. Ross. 'My fault Mrs. White. Susan, to glean is to obtain, collect, gather, or assemble, in dictionary terms. In practice, it is for one to gain information from another. Let me give you an example; Suppose you had the coin in a pendant around your neck, someone notices it and asks quite innocently; That's a nice pendant and very unusual, where did you get it? That is when you must be on your guard, anyone who shows an interest could be a fortune hunter. You could foil them by saying that you believe it is a replica of a museum piece given to you by a friend. It is not completely a lie but an uncertainty, I am a friend to you and I am uncertain about the validity of these coins because none here are experts in these matters. We can take nothing for granted Susan. Yes, it has been a very exciting day for us, but all might not be as it seems. The experts can tell us if we are fools with a haul of fakes intended to attract attention to this part of the coast. Shall we be secret fools or fools in the public eye? Fools loud and clear! Who then would respect The Coastal Guardians of which you are a member.

You Susan, your mother and father, Doris, me and my children, the Moran brothers, and Mr. Parker. All of us are The Coastal Guardians and many others who care for this coast but do not realise that they have us as their allies. We must and will, extend our helping hands to the villages and towns along our coast. Michael and James have made that clear to me with their emotional pleas on so many occasions. There can be none who love this coast more than me or my sons. Come back next year my friends, if not for my sake but for my sons and the strong friendships we share that shall last a lifetime, they will certainly last for mine.'

'Your words are most endearing to us city dwellers and we shall do as you ask because we feel at home here. I am sorry for the businesses who refused my professional services and denied me a reason to move here with my family. I could buy a cottage above the estuary and see what you enjoy each day as you look out from your windows. But I cannot do that without the promise of work, I have children to feed, clothe, and educate—' said Mr. White.

'You must discuss this with your family first, how do your wife and children feel about this sudden revelation? If you all agree, I can speak with those I might influence. You did reduce my home insurance by at least a third and that was six years ago. If you are serious about moving here to the coast I might be able to help. Have you considered how Susan and Chalky will feel, I mean, leaving the friends they have in London? Starting at a new school is not easy especially if it is mid-term. I can see that it is your dream, but is it theirs? Talk to them and get their views, tell them what it means to you to leave the city and join us country bumpkins, coastal tramps, or one of the many titles given to us by those who do not know us. We are thick-skinned, and sometimes thick-skulled because we do not care how the world sees us. We have a very close-knit community upon these lofty, windswept cliff-tops. It is home to us my friend and home is where the heart is. I can see that your heart is here ... you have three other hearts to consider besides your own, so talk with them and then talk with me and I will do all in my power to help you.

★ ★ ★

Later that evening in the holiday cottage on Clifftop Lane, Mr. White spoke with his family as his friend Peter Ross had suggested. His wife and daughter jumped at the idea of living on the coast, but Chalky had reservations. He loved the idea of living in this idyllic town, sailing with his friends, swimming, diving whenever the weather allowed … However, his first love was cricket, and his place on the school team was very important to him. A new school may not regard him with the same opinions as his school in London. And Chalky was just a year younger than Michael, but he felt his friend better educated than himself, he had shown that earlier in the day. He voiced his concerns to his family—

'It could well be that the school here is better at teaching, and of course, it will be a wrench for us all if we move here. We will be leaving everything we have grown-up with. If you decide that you cannot take that step I will understand and we will stay in London. When Susan is older and decides to live her own life away from us, your mother and I will move here if she agrees at that time,' said Chalky's father. 'If it will help you to decide, we will visit the local school and you can come with me to meet the teachers and discuss what facilities are available for students, they have an open day on Friday and I think we should go as a family. We can each ask the questions we have about your education, the opportunities for you both and so-forth. Peter and Doris are very active in the parent and teacher groups at the school. Peter is on the town council and he knows the people to influence, he has connections with the coastguards, the marine authorities … he amazes me with his workload and how calmly he deals with it all; he is a man to look-up to, an inspiration to me at least—'

'If I can get onto the cricket team I will not object, Dad,' Chalky said.

'Is that your only concern? What about your friends at school, your piano lessons, and the drama group?' said Mr. White.

'Mrs. Ross has a piano in her house and she used to teach music. Mike and Jamie are in the school play this Christmas, they told me so! At my school, they say I am the best cricketer in my year, but I might not be in a new school,' Chalky replied.

'So, this is about reputation. I have a good reputation at my company, but it does not make me happy. Let me tell you son; when your mother and I met I was an accountant, I held a senior position because I am good with numbers. Based on that skill, I moved to the insurance company I work for now. They pay me far more than I earned before and for that reason, we can afford to live in London. I know that I cannot earn here what London pays me, but life must be about more than money and what it can buy. I have no idea what Mr. Ross earns, and it is not my business to ask. He has his boat, his boys have their boat, and boats are not cheap to support, and they must pay insurance on them, mooring fees at the harbour ... I don't know how he manages. If we decide to live here I must have some serious discussions with him, but first, we must all agree to take that step. Let us visit the school, discuss our concerns with Peter and Doris because they live here and can guide us, we might be worrying for nothing.'

★ ★ ★

Mike and Jamie heard the discussions between the White family and their parents ...

'Chalky, this is the best place to live in the whole country. My school will welcome you with open arms if you are as good at cricket as you stated. We need good batsmen to boost our school, but we need good bowlers as well,' said Jamie.

'What about you Sue? Would you be happy to leave your friends in London to join us here?' asked Mike.

'You are good friends with us and I feel sure that your friends will soon become ours. We don't have many friends except some in our street ... and even some of those I don't like. I haven't met anyone here who I don't like, except that man at the castle who was a smuggler, the one you trapped and caught. Chalky and I played a very small part because the two of you took all the risks,' Susan said, referring to "The Mysterious Man."

'Sue, when we go out, it is my responsibility to look out for you and I try my best to do that. You can be head-strong at times, you tend not to think before you speak or act ... You have a strong will and we can see that, but you do not have the advantage of patience which my brother and I have. Dad taught us patience and he can teach it to you if you come to live here ... won't you Dad?' implored Mike.

'I certainly will. I will teach all the skills I have and welcome this family to our small stitch upon the quilted landscape that calls itself England. This is a proud coast, and we are a small town that has big ambitions. Join us and be part of the growth and reputation of this town. There might be many adventures ahead of us that can bring great accolades to this current backwater that few know of. You visit year upon year, is it because the town draws you back?' asked Mr. Ross.

'We so enjoy the company of the friends we have made here. Everyone is so welcoming and eager to help. We sometimes find a friendliness in London but not like it is here. This place is a world apart from where we live … but I must have work, Peter. I must earn a living to support my family and that is what holds me back from what I wish to do—' Mr. White began until Peter interrupted him.

'You have a fine house in London, good schools for your children, a well-paid job in the capital city, and yet you choose this sleepy backwater that few know of. I understand how this coast might draw you to its charms, it is so different here to what you are accustomed to. The silence can make you think you have turned deaf at times, the ocean's roars can deafen you. This is not London, this is a coast you enjoy in the summer months. Winter is harsh here, vicious, cold biting winds can tear the clothing from you. It is beautiful and idyllic in spring, summer, and at times in autumn. But winter is another story. Think hard my friend, because what is normal for us might present problems for you. All of that aside, are you diving with us tomorrow?' asked Peter Ross.

'We shall dive, and Susan will watch and wish with an eager heart.'

The End

Lightning Source UK Ltd.
Milton Keynes UK
UKOW01f1338060318
318972UK00001B/40/P

9 781546 289296